llama llama
holiday helper

Anna Dewdney

Based on the bestselling children's book series by Anna Dewdney

PENGUIN YOUNG READERS LICENSES
An Imprint of Penguin Random House LLC, New York

Copyright © Anna E. Dewdney Literary Trust. Copyright © 2020 Genius Brands International, Inc.
Published by Penguin Young Readers Licenses, an imprint of Penguin Random House LLC, New York. Manufactured in China.

Visit us online at www.penguinrandomhouse.com.

ISBN 9780593222591   10 9 8 7 6 5 4 3 2

llama llama
holiday helper

Anna Dewdney

Based on the bestselling children's book series by Anna Dewdney

Illustrated by JJ Harrison

Llama Llama drapes the last piece of tinsel on the tree. "There!" He steps back to hold Mama Llama's hand. "All done!"

Mama Llama smiles and looks around. "You have been such a good helper that we are ready for Christmas early!"

After snack time, Llama shakes the snow globes and restacks the presents.

Then he sits down and announces, "I'm bored!"

"Hmmm." Mama Llama pats him on the head. "Maybe others need help getting ready for the holidays."

"Good idea!" says Llama. "I'll go to Gram and Grandpa's first."

Gram pulls up on the tractor, wreaths piled high.
"You are just in time!" she says.
"We need your help."

Llama holds the wreaths as Grandpa
nails them to the fence.

Llama hugs his grandparents
before jumping back on his
scooter.

He pushes off, singing.

Holidays are so much fun.
I'm happy helping everyone!

Gilroy is setting up decorations outside. But the reindeer keep falling over!

Llama has an idea. "Let's put rocks around their hooves."

As they work, he asks, "What do you love about the holidays, Gilroy?"

"Getting presents!" his friend admits.

"And *this* year, I will remember to thank everyone!" Llama nods and smiles, thinking of the gifts he made for his friends.

"See you later!" Llama waves goodbye.

Holidays are so much fun.
I'm happy helping everyone!

Llama knocks at Nelly Gnu's back door.
"Do you need any help?" he asks.

"Yes!" Nelly hands him an apron. "We are baking cookies for Daddy Gnu's Bakery *and* our family."

While the cookies are in the oven, Nelly and Llama cut paper snowflakes. Suddenly, Llama sniffs and says, "The cookies smell ready!"

Daddy Gnu rushes in. "Just in time! Thank you, Llama!" They each try the cookies before Llama leaves.

At Euclid's, Llama's friend waves him in. "I just built this electric Yule log from a kit," says Euclid. Then he frowns. "But it doesn't work!"

Llama scratches his head. "Did you flip the switch to *on*?"
Euclid pushes the switch, and fake flames glow brightly.
"Sometimes I forget the easiest step. Thanks for reminding me!"

"You're welcome!" says Llama.
He laughs and sets off for Luna's house.

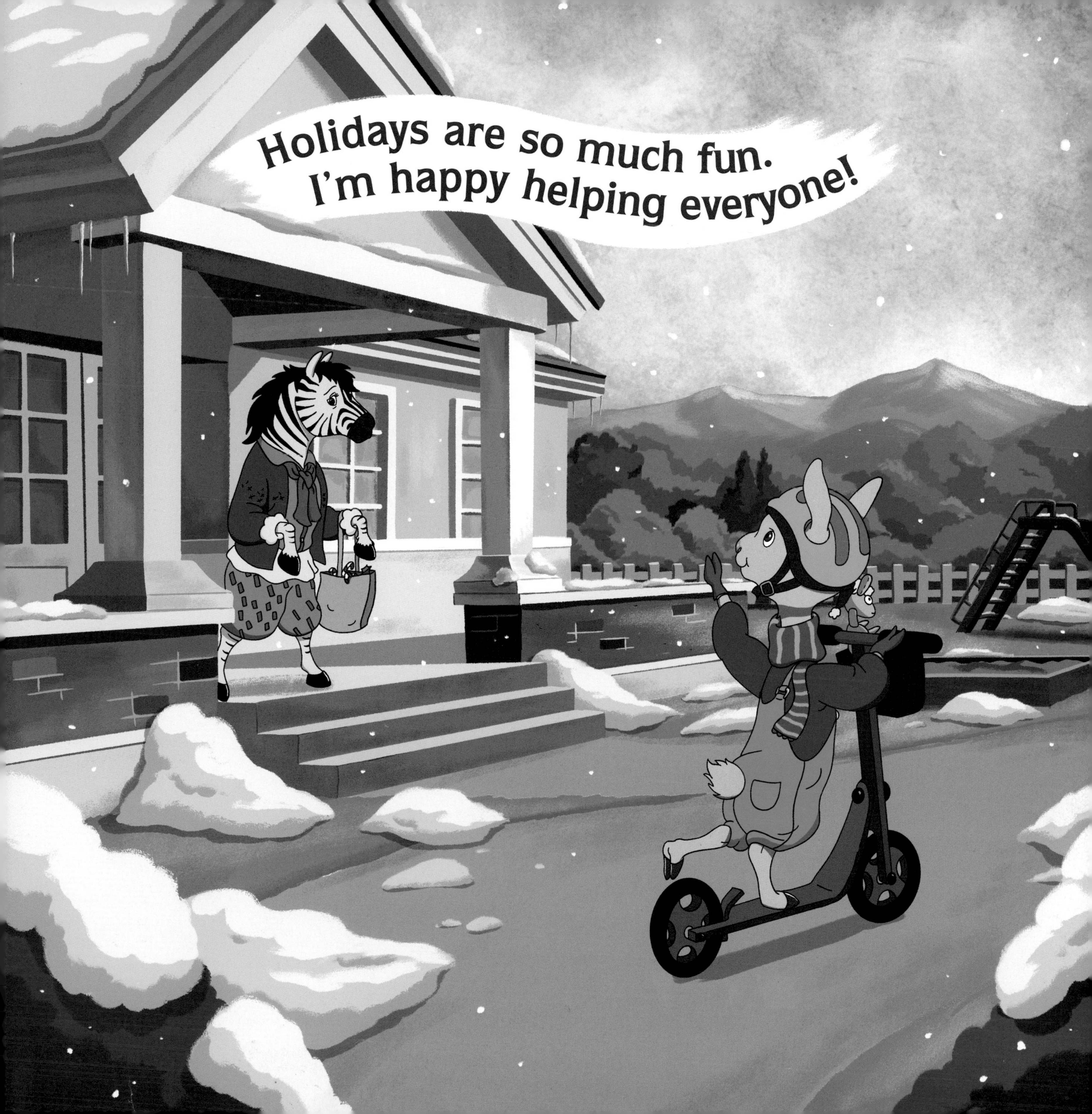

Holidays are so much fun.
I'm happy helping everyone!

Luna clears a spot for Llama at her craft table. "I'm making a centerpiece. Will you glue on the pine cones?"
"Sure!" says Llama.
Luna hums holiday songs as they finish. "Can you come caroling later?" she asks. "Everybody's going."
"I think so," Llama says. "Why don't you all stop at my house first?"

Llama hurries home.

Later, when he hears "Jingle Bells" being sung outside, Llama rushes to the window. But he trips on the light cord!

CRASH!

Tinkle! Tinkle!
Tink...
tink... tinkle...

"Oh no!" cries Llama.

DING-DONG!

"Help!" calls Llama.
His friends rush in.

"What a mess!" Llama moans. "Everything was perfect! The tree, the ornaments . . ."

"No worries," Nelly tells him. "Now *we* will help *you*!"

Together, they all stand up the tree.
Mama Llama sweeps up the broken bits.
Then Llama says, "Now let's open presents!"

His friends love their new wristbands. "Thank you!" they chorus
before handing him their gifts.

"New ornaments—just what I need!" Llama exclaims. "Thanks!"
"Let's hang them before we go caroling," suggests Luna.

Llama raises his mug of hot chocolate.

Today I'm glad for everyone
who's sharing Llama Llama fun!
Happy holidays!